CAPTAIN SCARLET

MYSTERON TRAP

BY GRAHAM MARKS

Adapted from the TV story
The Inquisition

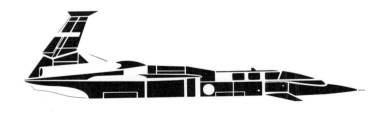

BOXTREE

In the year 2068 a team from Spectrum, Earth's worldwide security agency, landed on the the planet Mars. The expedition was led by Captain Black.

A highly advanced Martian race, the Mysterons, saw the landing as an invasion and launched their own attack. Capturing and recruiting Captain Black as a Mysteron agent they returned him to Earth.

The Mysterons have the power to regenerate a person killed in conflict. This same power has also made Spectrum agent Captain Scarlet indestructible.

Spectrum and Captain Scarlet now lead the fight against Captain black and the Mysterons. The fate of the planet now rests in their hands...

Even Spectrum agents have to have some time off to relax and enjoy themselves, and tonight was the night that Captain Blue and Captain Scarlet had decided to go to one of their favourite restaurants.

'Did you enjoy the meal, sir?' asked their waiter as he cleared the table.

'Very much,' replied Captain Blue. 'Could you bring me a black coffee, please?'

'Nothing for me,' Captain Scarlet told the waiter.

While Captain Blue drank his coffee, both men listened to the pianist playing a slow jazz number. He was well known in the area and the two friends really liked his music. But, quite suddenly, Captain Blue began to feel extremely woozy and his eyelids felt very heavy.

'Are you feeling all right, Adam?' enquired Captain Scarlet.

'No...no I don't...' mumbled the captain. 'That coffee, it tasted odd...'

'Stay right there,' Captain Scarlet got up as his friend slumped back in his chair. 'I'll go and get our coats.'

Returning from the cloakroom, Captain Scarlet saw their table was empty. Looking round the restaurant he could see no sign of Captain Blue. It was as if he had disappeared into thin air!

Slowly Captain Blue's head cleared. There was a ringing in his ears and when he tried to open his eyes he couldn't see very well, but what he could make out looked like the Control Room on Cloudbase.

'Where am I?' he muttered to himself.

'Don't you know?' said a voice he didn't recognise. He turned, blinking his eyes, to see who had spoken. A stranger was sitting in Colonel White's chair.

'This is Cloudbase, and I am Cogan, Spectrum Intelligence...' replied the man. 'But more to the point, who are you?'

Cogan went on to ask the dazed Captain Blue where he'd been for the last three months, demanding to know if he could prove who he was by telling him the cypher codes. Captain Blue refused point blank. Cogan then asked him about the Spectrum mission to destroy the Mysteron Base on the moon.

'I suppose it can't do any harm,' frowned Captain Blue, sitting back. 'Captain Scarlet, Lieutenant Green and I had gone to Crater 101. We had until midnight to explore the complex before a bomb, being taken there on a transporter tank by an operative from the Lunar Base, was due to explode...'

'The Mysteron base was incredible,' Captain Blue told Cogan. 'Like nothing I'd ever seen before! It filled Crater 101, and every building glowed with strange and beautiful coloured lights.

'We went inside to find it deserted but still operational, but what we didn't know was that the Mysterons had turned the tank driver into one of their agents. He had set the bomb to go off at 10 o'clock!'

Captain Blue went on to describe how the controller at the Lunar Base had discovered what was going on, but had been unable to contact the recce party at the complex because they were below the lunar horizon and out of radio contact.

'The controller went straight to the base commander and told him what had happened,' Captain Blue said. 'He was a quick-thinking man and knew immediately that the only chance of getting a message to Captain Scarlet was by launching an unmanned rocket, programmed to land just inside the crater. The controller insisted it must be one of the few old CB-29s left on the base.

'Working at lightning speed technicians got the rocket ready for take-off and an immediate countdown was ordered. As the slim silver missile blasted off, all the crew of the Lunar Base could do was hope that it arrived on time.'

'We were walking through the strangely shaped main building when Captain Scarlet told us to wait,' Captain Blue continued with his story. 'He had discovered some kind of weightless area and was beginning to rise up off the ground.'

'Go on,' smiled Cogan. 'This is all very interesting.'

'As he floated upwards he radioed back down that it was OK for us to follow him,' said the Captain. 'It was while Lieutenant Green and myself were in mid-air that Captain Scarlet told us he thought he'd found the heart of the complex.'

Leaning forward in his chair, Captain Blue stopped talking and stared thoughtfully into the middle distance.

'On the far side of the room we'd come in to was something that looked almost like an altar,' he went on. 'In the centre of the thing there was a large crystal, turning round and round as we looked at it. All my instruments were going crazy, and it was then that I knew we'd found the power source!

'As Lieutenant Green took pictures, Captain Scarlet got out a pair of long pincers and began to try and remove the crystal. It was then we heard the rocket crash land outside, and I went to a window and saw it was an old CB-29.'

'We couldn't work out what the heck the guys at Lunar Base were doing launching an obslete rocket like the CB-29,' Captain Blue told Cogan. The man just nodded, as if to say 'Carry on'. So the captain did.

He told him that at first they thought it might contain a message, but then Captain Scarlet realised it could be a warning. He remembered the flight controller at Lunarville 6 giving him a memento of the CB29 Neptune mission in 2058 as a lucky charm. On it was an inscription which read 'We made it - ahead of schedule!'. In a flash he worked out it could mean tthe bomb was going to go off sooner than they thought.

'I went straight outside to check the detonator,' continued Captain Blue. 'And Captain Scarlet sent Green back to the moon mobile while he carried on trying to disconnect the crystal power source. He said he'd follow us in the lunar tractor as soon as he'd finished.

'When I got outside, I found that Captain Scarlet was right,' Captain Blue held up one hand. 'There were only five minutes left on the counter! Lieutenant Green and I could do nothing else but follow our orders and leave in the moon mobile, hoping that Scarlet had enough time left to get out safely.'

'Captain Scarlet told me later that even he didn't think he'd get out of the complex unscathed,' Captain Blue looked straight at Cogan. 'The crystal seemed to be fixed in place by some kind of force field, and he couldn't loosen it.'

'He must be a very brave man,' said Cogan. 'Either that or very foolish.'

'There's nothing foolish about bravery!' snapped Captain Blue. 'Especially not the kind displayed by a man like Captain Scarlet.'

'Absolutely!' smiled Cogan. 'I was just testing your loyalty. Go on...'

Captain Blue wanted to hit him, but that would do nothing to prove his identity. He went on to tell Cogan that he and Lieutenant Green had driven the moon mobile out of the crater not knowing if they'd ever see Captain Scarlet again.

'At any moment we expected the yellow lunar tractor to come over the crater lip, but all we saw was the orange mushroom cloud blossoming against the black sky as the nuclear bomb exploded.

'Then, as the complex itself blew up, the lunar tank appeared, almost as if it was thrown out by the explosion. Captain Scarlet had made it, just in time, and with the power source intact.'

'A nice story, Captain Blue...if that's who you really are,' smirked Cogan. 'But as it was in all the papers when it happened, you could merely have added a few details.'

'I was there!' shouted Captain Blue. 'I demand to see Colonel White!' 'All in good time!' replied Cogan. 'I'm not satisfied yet. I need something more substantial. If you are Captain Blue it shouldn't be so difficult to prove it.'

'Wait a minute!' Captain Blue thumped the arm of his chair. 'There was a conference at Glengarry Castle, but the story was never released to the press. It's only Class C security, so I can tell you - this should prove my identity beyond any reasonable doubt!'

Captain Blue, relaxing a little, told Cogan that the delegates to the conference were the top brass of the World Airforce. Captain Scarlet had been checking the castle out when he discovered a machine-gun nest in a secret cubby-hole behind a large portrait in the main meeting room.

Before he could do anything about it he was captured and tied up by Goddard, the man in charge of setting the conference up. Goddard had been turned into a Mysteron agent who planned to assassinate the entire Supreme Command of the World Airforce.

'There was nothing that Captain Scarlet could do,' said Captain Blue. 'He was bound and gagged to a chair, knowing that disaster would strike in a few hours' time. He told me later he nearly ripped his hands off trying to get free. He only just made it in time.

'As the clock was about to strike ten, Captain Scarlet burst into the conference room and sprayed the hidden cubby-hole with bullets, killing the assassin.' Captain Blue took a deep breath. 'It was all over in seconds and no one else was injured, but in the confusion of getting the top brass out to the magnicopter Goddard escaped.'

'What happened next?' asked the security man, leaning forward. 'Where were you when all this was going on?'

'I was outside in a Spectrum Pursuit Vehicle, scanning the castle with binoculars,' continued the captain. 'I spotted Goddard on the battlements with a high-powered machine-gun and realised there was no way the magnicopter could take off without being in his line of fire. The whole of the Supreme Command was trapped - we had to get to him, and quick!'

'Captain Scarlet got out of the castle and took the hoversuit out of the SPV,' Captain Blue could see everything in his mind's eye, as clearly as if he was still there. 'He told me to cover him with the SPV rocket and went after Goddard.' Captain Blue described how his fellow agent powered up, and that as soon as he was airborne Goddard had sent a hail of gunfire his way. It was a miracle that he hadn't been hit. As soon as he'd landed on the battlements, Captain Scarlet radioed to the magnicopter that he was going to divert the Mysteron agent's attention. They were to take off as soon as the coast was clear.

'Was it as easy as that?' enquired Cogan. 'The Mysterons are usually harder to foil.'

'It's never easy,' said Captain Blue. 'Goddard's machine-gun was extremely powerful, and Captain Scarlet was badly hit as he tried to get to him. My orders were, no matter what, to fire a rocket at Goddard as soon as the magnicopter was out of the way.'

'Surely you might have hit Captain Scarlet as well!' Cogan said.

'True,' replied Captain Blue. 'But a Spectrum agent always obeys orders, you should know that...if you are one...'

'It's not my identity we're talking about,' smiled Cogan. 'You still haven't proved who you are. Now if you were to tell me the Spectrum cipher codes...'

'You know I can't do that!' said Captain Blue, suddenly spotting something on Colonel White's desk. 'Is that my file?'

'It's Captain Blue's file,' replied Cogan. 'And you do look like the man in the photo, but plastic surgery can work wonders - why don't you just tell me the cipher codes?'

'Check my fingerprints!' demanded Captain Blue, getting up. 'They can't be altered!'

'I'm tired of this cat-and-mouse game, Captain...'

'You called me by my rank!' Captain Blue moved forward towards the desk. 'You do know who I am! I've had enough of this - I'm getting out of here!'

Turning, Captain Blue ran for the door. As he did so alarm sirens went off and the door opened to reveal another man who was hold-ing a gun in one hand and a hypodermic syringe in the other.

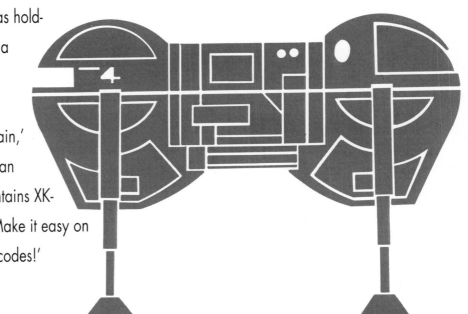

'Don't try anything, Captain,' said Cogan, as the other man advanced. 'The syringe contains XK-4, the ultimate truth drug. Make it easy on yourself, tell me the cipher codes!'

'Go take a walk!' sneered Captain Blue, suddenly turning and running straight at the window of Cloudbase's control room. 'I'd rather die than tell you anything!'

Cogan and his associate looked on in amazement as Captain Blue crashed right through the glass and out into space.

But as he hit the ground, only a few feet below the smashed window, Captain Blue's mind was racing. He should be dead, not lying on the rough concrete floor of a derelict warehouse. And then he heard a voice.

'Get up, Captain Blue!' it said. The captain looked out of the open warehouse door to see Captain Scarlet getting out of an SPV and beckoning him.

Captain Blue needed no more urging. He ran for his life out towards the SPV, and as soon as he'd reached it the driver fired a rocket into the warehouse. There was a huge explosion, and the fake Cloudbase burst into flames.

'The Mysterons boasted that a member of Spectrum would betray us,' Captain Scarlet told his friend. 'It took a few hours to find you, but we made it just in time!'

'They nearly had me fooled,' said Captain Blue. 'But a Spectrum agent never betrays his colleagues!'

First published in the UK 1993 by BOXTREE LTD, Broadwall House, 21 Broadwall,
London SE1 9PL
1 3 5 7 9 10 8 6 4 2
Copyright © 1993 ITC ENTERTAINMENT GROUP LTD.
Licensed by Copyright Promotions Ltd.
Design and illustrations by Arkadia
1-85283-864-7